Oksana
MY OWN STORY

With special thanks to Galina Zmievskaya, Viktor and Nina Petrenko, Michael Carlisle, Heather Alexander, Sarah Hall, Debra Goldstein, and Joseph Lemire.

PRODUCED AND CREATED BY PARACHUTE PRESS, INC.

Photography credits: Oksana Baiul (p 8, 9, 10, 13, 14, 15, 16, 17, 19, 21); DUOMO/Rick Rickman (p 34); Focus On Sports Inc. (p 31, 37, 39); Michelle Harvath (back cover); Paul Harvath (front cover, p 24, 33, 45 left); Nikolai Ignatiev/Network Matrix (p 23, 25); Daniel Hill/Outline (p 46); Parachute Press, Inc. (p 32, 45 right); Betty Marshall/Shooting Star (p 7, 44); SportsChrome (half title); Bill Eppridge/Sports Illustrated (p 41); Heinz Kluetmeier/Sports Illustrated (p 6, 27, 42); Manny Millan/Sports Illustrated (title page, p 30); Caron/Sygma (p 40, 43); Forestier/Sygma (p 28, 35). Special thanks to Elaine Ubina/UV Studios for the backstage photos.

For information on how to join the official Oksana Baiul Fan Club, please write to: Oksana Baiul Fan Club, c/o Fan Emporium, P.O. Box 679 Branford, CT 06405

DESIGNED BY MICHELE ITALIANO-PERLA

http://www.randomhouse.com

Library of Congress Catalog Number: 96-69537
ISBN: 0-679-88382-7
Printed in the United States of America
10 9 8 7 6 5 4 3 2 1

Oksana

MY OWN

By Oksana

as told to Hea

RANDOM HOUSE

Dear Friend,

I am so happy that you want to read my story!

I have worked hard at my skating for many years, but I could not have done it without the help of my coaches and friends — and fans like you. Your smiles, your applause, and your cheers lift my heart as I skate. I skate for you, and for myself, but also for my beloved family.

When the gold medal was placed around my neck at the 1994 Olympic Games, I burst into tears of happiness. But I was sad too, because my dear Mama and my grandparents had died before they could see this special day. Still, I knew somehow that they were there with me on the ice in Norway. Their love helped give me the strength to fight for my Olypmic dream.

I do not know where the future will lead me. But I do know one thing. I cannot imagine my life away from the ice!

Yours,

Oksana

When I was a little girl in Ukraine, Mama asked me if I would skate to the music from her favorite ballet, *Swan Lake*.

"I can't, Mama," I told her. "The music is too slow. I want to skate to something I can do a lot of jumps to."

"Someday you will understand the music, Oksana," Mama said. "Someday you will skate to *Swan Lake*."

Mama was right. I did skate to *Swan Lake* at the 1994 Olympics. As I skated, I felt that I was telling a story about me. A story that proves how, with love and hard work, fairy tales really can come true . . . .

I was born on November 16, 1977, in a Ukraine factory town called Dnepropetrovsk. My mother, Marina, and I lived in a small three-room apartment. I never really knew my father, Sergei. He left us when I was two years old, and my family never saw him again. But my grandmother and my

Here I am at age one. Even back then I loved to smile for the camera!

grandfather lived with Mama and me. All three of them made my childhood a happy one.

While Mama worked, teaching French in the local school, my grandmother — or *babushka* in Russian — stayed home with me. Babushka would tell me many stories about Mama when she was a young girl.

Mama had been a dancer, and she wanted me to become a dancer too. I would twirl around our tiny apartment, and Mama would clap her hands in delight. "Oksana," she would say, "you will grow up to be a beautiful ballerina!"

"You will grow up to be a beautiful ballerina!" Mama told me.

But just before my fourth birthday, my grandfather told Mama, "Oksana is too fat. No ballet school will take her."

Mama was heartbroken. But Grandfather smiled at me. "Don't worry, Oksana," he said, "I have brought you a very special present." Then he handed me a large box.

I quickly opened it. "Ice skates!" I exclaimed in surprise.

"Oksana should figure skate," Grandfather told Mama. "Skating will help her lose weight for ballet."

The skates were not brand-new, but I did not care. I gazed with pleasure at their gleaming white leather and shiny silver blades. The next day, Grandfather took me to the ice rink in our town. From the moment I stepped on the ice, I loved skating. Around me, the other kids slipped, slided, and fell. Not me! I skated faster and faster. I never wanted to stop!

When I was seven, my skating coach was Stanislav Korytek. He was strict but very kind. He entered me in my first local competition. The night before, Mama showed me

the beautiful, bright green skating dress I would wear. But I did not smile.

"What's wrong, Oksana?" Mama asked.

"I'm scared," I answered. "Oh, Mama, what if I fall down in front of everyone?"

"It won't matter if you fall," Mama told me. "Remember what Coach Stanislav says. Always smile when you are on the ice, and have a good time. Then everything will be all right."

It worked! I smiled and I didn't fall. I won my very first competition. And it was fun!

I was no longer a chubby little girl. Skating had made me thin and strong. After the competition, Mama asked me if I wanted to go to ballet school. At that time in the Soviet Union, ballerinas began training at age seven. It was then or never.

"No," I told Mama. "I want to keep on skating. I don't *ever* want to do anything else!"

There weren't many girls in my town who skated, so I always practiced with the boys. My best friend, Slavik, was the same age as me. We always skated together. I had so much energy, I could skate faster and jump higher than Slavik. But I would also fall really, really hard!

When I was only nine years old, I landed my first triple jump, a triple Lutz. Slavik couldn't believe it! The Lutz is the hardest triple for most skaters. But for some reason it came easily to me. It is still my favorite jump. I always try to perform the triple Lutz first in my programs.

It took me many more months to land the double Axel,

LEFT: Here I am at age four in the skates my grandfather bought me. The ice rink in my hometown was always very cold, so Mama bundled me up in many layers of clothes.

which most skaters master *before* they begin to do triples! I have no idea why this jump was so hard for me. Even now I don't like doing double Axels very much!

Those years were filled with happy memories. I would skate in the early morning, and attend school with my friends. Afterward, I would skate again, then visit with Grandfather in the park. He would walk me home to Mama and Babushka. But when I was ten, my life began to change. My grandfather died unexpectedly. I missed him terribly, especially his funny stories and jokes. Now I came straight home from the rink alone. The apartment seemed very quiet without him.

Less than a year later, Babushka became ill and died. I felt so lost without her. She left me her gold cross necklace. Every night I would touch the necklace for comfort. Mama and I would hug each other and cry ourselves to sleep.

Now Mama was the center of my world. And she was thrilled that I loved skating more and more. I remember watching the 1988 Winter Olympics on TV with Slavik. Katarina Witt, Brian Boitano, and Jill Trenary were the first Olympic skaters I had ever seen. They were spectacular!

I spent hours telling Mama all about them. One night, as I climbed into bed, I asked, "Do you think I'll ever skate like that? If I work really, really hard?"

Mama smoothed back my hair and kissed me.

"Oksana," she said, "you will be a great skater. I feel it in my heart. You must follow your dream."

For the next three years I worked very hard. Mama married my stepfather, Turek, and we were all happy. But as in all fairy tales, there was great sadness ahead. Something terrible was about to happen. It would change my life forever.

Mama and me in the park where my grandfather used to work.

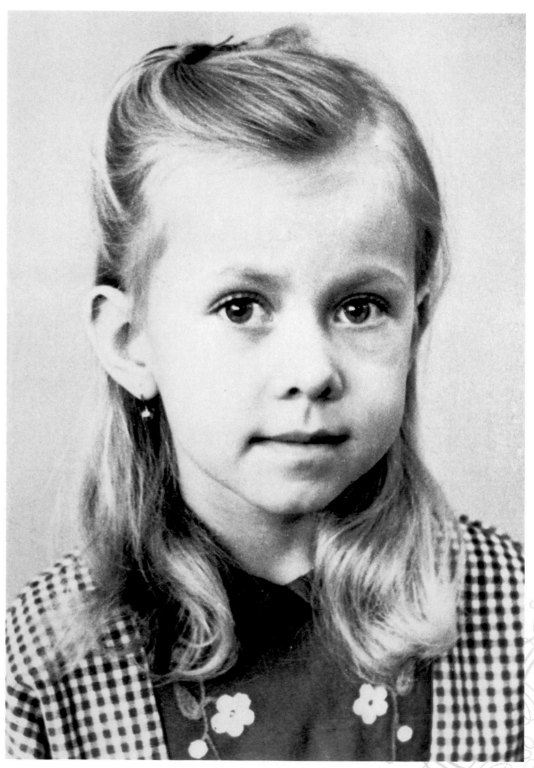

This is my class photo from elementary school when I was six years old.
Mama made the dress I was wearing. It was my favorite!

I knew immediately that the news was bad — very bad. It was an August afternoon in 1991. I was thirteen. I was on the ice practicing when Coach Stanislav called me to the side of the rink. "Oksana," he said softly, "it's your mama."

This is my Mama— Marina Baiul.

I felt my heart stop. The tone of his voice told me everything I needed to know. Mama — my beautiful Mama — had died.

I could not stop crying.

I knew that Mama had cancer. She had not been feeling well for many months. But I had no idea she had such a short time left to live. Her doctor told me the cancer had spread very quickly. Mama did not want me to know. She did not want to upset me.

I sat alone at Mama's funeral. I could not speak to anyone. I did not know what to do next or where to go. How could I live without her? I felt that I barely knew my stepfather. With tears streaming down my face, I ran to the one place that still felt like home: the ice rink.

It was nighttime when Coach Stanislav found me at the rink. He took me to his house to live with his wife and baby daughter.

The Koryteks were very kind to me, but I missed Mama so, so much. Every night I fell asleep thinking about her. Every morning I awoke, picturing her smiling face. The only time I found happiness was at the ice rink, practicing with my coach and Slavik.

I practiced my skating harder than ever. In the evenings, my muscles ached. My legs were covered with huge bruises from constantly falling. But I was determined to follow my dream to be the best. Someday, I would go to the Olympics and win a gold medal. I would win it for Mama.

I was still very young and new to the world of competitive skating. I needed to win a major competition to be taken seriously. And, in November 1991, I got my chance at a big competition in Moscow. Then Coach Stanislav told me he couldn't go with me.

"But you have to!" I cried. "I've never gone to a competition without you! This one is so important!"

"I am sorry, Oksana," Stanislav said quietly. "Don't worry. You will do fine without me."

I skated horribly in practice that afternoon. I told Slavik that I could not go to the competition alone. I was too afraid.

"I have a great idea," Slavik said. "I'll go to the competition with you. Then you won't be alone!"

Even at age five, I pretended to be a ballerina on the ice.

At the competition, the stands were filled with people. I was so nervous! Finally my name was called over the loudspeaker. I skated slowly to the center of the ice. I glanced into the stands and Slavik waved to me. I smiled.

My music began, and I pushed off into my program. I did not make a single mistake.

"I won! Coach Stanislav, I won!" I cried as I raced into the ice rink back in Dnepropetrovsk the next day. I couldn't wait to show him my gold medal. But to my surprise, his office was dark and empty.

A proud moment for me and two skaters from my hometown. We had just won a local competition. I'm the one in the middle!

Coach Stanislav wasn't at home either. His wife said that he had taken a trip to Canada. We waited and waited. But he didn't come back. We finally learned that he had a new job and a whole new life in Canada. He was never coming home.

Never coming home? How could he leave without telling me? I was devastated. I raced to the rink and threw my skates into the trash. I vowed never to skate again.

I moved back to my stepfather's apartment. I tried to avoid the ice rink. But in my town there was only one route to school — and it took me right by the rink. The first week I didn't even look up as I passed. The second week I slowed down, but I forced myself to walk on.

The third week arrived. I found myself in front of the rink. I missed skating so much! It felt as though my heart would break. I had to go inside.

I rushed into the rink — and stopped short. I had thrown away my only pair of skates!

"Surprise!" Slavik shouted. He held up my battered skates. "I pulled these out of the trash weeks ago," he told me. "I knew you could never stop skating."

He was right.

I continued to compete, even without a coach. That winter I finished in a disappointing twelfth place at the Soviet Championships. That summer I went to the annual meeting of the Ukrainian Skating Federation, where skaters

RIGHT: I was always very nervous when I competed. But picturing Mama's smiling face gave me courage.

and their coaches make plans for the following year of competitions. Alone and scared, I met Valentine Nicolaj, a well-known skating coach.

"I have seen you skate," Valentine told me. "You should move to Odessa. You could train with me and Galina Zmievskaya."

"Galina Zmievskaya!" I shrieked in astonishment.

Everyone knew Galina. She was the best coach in Ukraine! She trained Viktor Petrenko, and that winter in Albertville, France, Viktor had won the 1992 Olympic gold medal. Why would Galina want to coach *me*? I only knew I had to go.

When I returned home, I packed my few belongings into a suitcase.

"I am moving to Odessa," I told my stepfather. "I am going there to skate."

"You're only fourteen," he protested. "Would your mama have wanted you to go?"

I knew that she would. After many discussions, Turek finally agreed that this was the right choice for me. I traveled the 250 miles to Odessa by train.

I was shocked when I arrived. The Odessa ice rink was in terrible condition. Green algae covered the soft, slushy ice, making skating dangerous. Often, the electricity was turned off, forcing skaters to practice in darkness. There was no Zamboni machine. If you wanted to clean the ice, you had to find the broom and shovel and do it yourself. The air was freezing cold. I had to wear three or four layers of clothes just to keep warm.

But I did not care. I had come to this rink to skate for Galina and to find out if I was good enough to be her student.

*I love performing to music. During practice sessions, I often made
up new routines—to other skaters' music!*

Galina was not in Odessa when I arrived. She was in America with Viktor on a big skating tour. For two weeks I worked only with Valentine. He was much more demanding than Coach Stanislav had been. My skating quickly improved.

One day I arrived at the rink and knew right away that something was different. "Galina is back!" all the skaters were whispering. I froze. Suddenly I was so nervous! Could I skate in front of such a famous coach?

Once again, I thought of Mama. She told me always to be brave. And I knew she was right.

I warmed up for about ten minutes. I glanced toward the wooden benches by the side of the rink. Galina sat there, talking with Viktor. Were they watching me? I wasn't sure.

I tried to keep my legs from shaking as I performed several double jumps.

"Let me see a camel spin!" Galina called.

A camel spin wasn't difficult for me. I stepped into the spin and arched my back. But somehow I lost my balance and fell! I heard laughter. First from Viktor, then from Galina. My face turned bright red. They were laughing at me!

Galina called me over. I was sure she would tell me to go back to Dnepropetrovsk. Instead, she said I was very talented. She offered to be my coach! She warned that I would have to work harder than I'd ever worked before. I couldn't wait to begin!

RIGHT: I liked living with Galina. We had fun, but we also had a lot of serious talks—especially about skating!

Galina invited me to live with her family. Her three-room apartment was already very crowded with her husband, Nicolai, her mother, Maria, and Nina and Galya, her two daughters. Nina had just married Viktor Petrenko and planned to move out, so I was given her old bed in the tiny room she had shared with Galya.

Living in Odessa was an enormous change for me, but the biggest change was working with Galina. I remember our first practice together. It was awful!

Galina Zmievskaya and me.

Galina played the music Stanislav had put together for me before he left. I had skated about half the routine when the music suddenly stopped.

"Where is your program?" Galina called.

"I just skated it," I replied.

"Where are the steps?" Galina asked.

"I did them," I said, confused.

"I did not see them," she told me. The next day Galina brought me new music — an upbeat medley of Broadway show tunes. In the next week she put together a whole new program. Then Galina said, "Okay. Now you are going to skate the program for me, but without the spins and without the jumps. Just the steps."

I had never done such a thing before. I began the program again. Halfway through I had to stop. I was completely out of breath! It was the hardest program I had ever skated — even without the difficult jumps and spins!

That was how Galina made me realize the importance of choreography. She taught me how to use my whole body — my arms, my hands, even the way I tilted my head — to tell a story and show emotion.

RIGHT: I spend many hours on the ice, but I always work for at least an hour each day on ballet. Ballet helps give my skating a graceful look.

Together, we worked and worked on my new program. Slowly it began to improve. Galina kept adding new elements to increase the difficulty. That was when she created my special spin. She had me stretch to grab hold of my left skate behind my head, curving my upper body into a circle.

At first, when I tried that position, the pain was so horrible that I would cry after practice. I never thought I could hold the position and build up the speed I needed to spin. But Galina believed in me. Soon I was able to do the spin. But I have to admit, even today it *still* hurts a bit!

I was glad to have my new spin in time for the Ukrainian National competition. The year before, I had finished in twelfth place. This year I had a new coach, a new program, a new style, and even new skates that Viktor Petrenko had bought for me. As I skated my program, I could feel Mama smiling down on me.

I won the competition! As the new national champion, I would soon represent Ukraine in Helsinki, Finland, at the European Championships. Now I worked extra hard on my program. I had only a short time left to practice, and I wanted my skating to be perfect. I wanted to show everyone the new Oksana.

Galina and I celebrated New Year's Eve with Viktor, Nina, and Galya. But the next morning, Galina did not feel well. A few hours later, she had a heart attack. She was rushed to the hospital.

The doctors told me that Galina would be okay, but how could I believe them? I had already lost almost everyone

RIGHT: Here I am performing my "special spin" during the 1994 Olympics.

Viktor Petrenko has been like a big brother to me. He bought me skates
when I was too poor to buy them myself. Now Viktor and I have so much
fun performing together.

I was ever close to. I refused to leave her bedside.

"Nonsense," Galina said. "You must leave. You must skate in the Europeans. Valentine will go with you as your coach. I will be thinking of you, Oksana. I am sure your mama will too."

Galina's words helped me. Still, as I entered the ice rink in Helsinki, I had to take a deep breath to calm my nerves. I was about to compete against the best skaters in Europe — the same skaters I had watched on television only a year before, including Surya Bonaly of France. Surya was famous for her amazing jump combinations. I was not famous at all!

I completed all the required elements in my short program without one mistake. But the competition wasn't over yet. Now I faced the long program, which counted for two-thirds of my final score.

The funny thing was, I did not feel very nervous. Nobody expected me to win a medal that day. But Galina had packed my program with difficult triple jumps. We both hoped that if I landed them all, I might do well.

The first notes of "The Rain in Spain" from *My Fair Lady* rang out. I skated with more speed and focus than ever before. The audience cheered for me, and I landed every one of my jumps cleanly.

When the scores were posted, I couldn't believe it. Surya had won the gold medal, and I had won the silver!

I was so proud. This medal was for Galina — and, as always, for Mama.

We three had won it together.

Two months later, Galina and I traveled to Prague, Czechoslovakia, for the 1993 World Championships. I was

competing against the top women skaters from Europe, the United States, Japan, and China. American Nancy Kerrigan was in first place after the short program. Nancy had already won the bronze medal at the 1992 Olympics in Albertville. But there was still the long program left. I knew I had to skate perfectly to beat her.

I wore a bright blue skating dress, patterned after the dress Jill Trenary wore in the 1988 Olympics. I completed five different triple jumps — and won the competition! At fifteen I was the youngest World Champion since Sonja

Here I am with Chen Lu of China, totally amazed that I am the 1993 World Champion!

LEFT: My long program at the 1993 World Championships in Prague—Galina taught me to use my whole body to tell a story on the ice.

Henie in 1927. Suddenly everyone knew who I was.

I love signing autographs and taking pictures with fans during ice shows— or anytime!

After Prague, the fun really began. I was invited to join the Tom Collins Tour of World Figure Skating Champions, which features the top amateur skaters in the world. For the first time, I flew to the United States.

The tour began in Las Vegas, Nevada. The lights, the noise, the glitter — I loved them all! America seemed like a fantasy land.

Still, as I waited backstage each night, I felt very, very nervous. My heart pounded fast and hard. One night I started crying. I was scared to death. I was terrified to skate in front of such a crowd — 20,000 people!

Brian Boitano, the 1988 Olympic men's gold medalist, walked me to a nearby bench and sat down next to me. "Oksana," he said, "you are an excellent skater. Those people out there are your friends. Skate for them like you would skate for your friends back home, and everything will be all right."

I thought of my dear friend Slavik, and I tried to skate for him. Brian's trick worked. Everything *was* all right. I always remember what he told me that night — because I am always nervous before I skate!

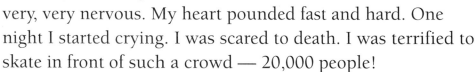

In 1993, I performed for the first time with the Tom Collins Tour of World Figure Skating Champions. I was the youngest skater on the tour!

When the tour was over, I headed to Sun Valley, Idaho, for the 1993 Sun Valley Competition. Galina and I walked through the pretty little town and talked about the upcoming season. The next World Championships — and the Olympics — were only one year away. Galina felt I now needed a stronger, more challenging short program. We strolled by a pond that was home to six or seven gorgeous swans. I remember pointing them out to Galina.

"*Swan Lake* was Mama's favorite ballet," I said. "She always wanted me to skate to Tchaikovsky's beautiful music."

"Perhaps now would be a good time," Galina said.

When we returned to Odessa, Galina and Nina Stoyan, my ballet teacher, began to choreograph my new short program. Nina was a very important ballet dancer in Ukraine. She felt that I should skate *Swan Lake* as if I were performing ballet. It was Nina's idea to have me walk on my toes as if I were dancing in toe shoes.

"No, no," Galina said. "She cannot! That is too hard to do on the ice."

But Nina insisted. "I do not want Oksana to look like everyone else. I want her to look special."

Whether it's a practice session or an important competition, I always know that Galina will be there there for me.

Finally, Galina agreed. I began practicing moving around the ice on my toe picks. At first my feet hurt so badly that I could hardly walk for days afterward. But I kept at it, and after a few weeks the pain disappeared.

I practiced my routine on the ice and in the ballet room. I had to be graceful, yet skate with enough power to land triple jump combinations. As I practiced, Galina would yell, "Don't be a cow! You are a swan! You are flying!"

Before I knew it, it was time to leave for the 1994 European Championships in Copenhagen, Denmark. I had grown over four inches in the past few months, and my new height made it hard for me to hold on to some of the combination jumps. Still, I again finished second to Surya Bonaly. I'd won another silver medal!

I won the silver medal at the 1994 European Championships. Surya Bonaly (middle) from France won the gold and Olga Markova (left) from Russia took the bronze.

I returned to Odessa to prepare for the biggest competition of all, the 1994 Winter Olympics. This was the moment I had been dreaming of and working for ever since I could remember.

In February, Galina and Valentine flew with me to Lillehammer, Norway. I had never been so excited! I knew my competition for the gold medal would come from Nancy Kerrigan, Surya Bonaly, and Chen Lu of China.

Galina warned me, "Do not think about the other skaters. Think only of becoming a swan on the ice."

My name was called to begin my short program. I waited a few seconds. Galina had always cautioned me not to rush onto the ice before I was ready. The judges would wait for me, she said. And I was ready to give them something worth waiting for.

I took a deep breath, skated around in a small circle, and assumed my opening pose. Finally, I heard the first few notes of the beautiful swan music.

I began the graceful, ballet-like moves across the ice. Then I prepared for the opening jump combination that would set the rhythm for the rest of my program. If I landed it well, I knew everything would be okay.

I gathered great speed, and launched myself into the air. I landed cleanly! I can remember smiling and skating forward with a burst of energy. Then I landed the jump that always gave me so much trouble — the double Axel!

All the time, I skated not as Oksana, but as the graceful black swan. And as the music died, so did the swan.

The crowd cheered, and I was filled with happiness. "I skated *Swan Lake*, Mama," I whispered. "I skated it for you."

I sat between Galina and Valentine as we waited for my

scores. The area that the skaters and their coaches sit in is often called the "kiss and cry." That day I did both. I finished in second place, behind Nancy Kerrigan. A lot of attention was being focused on Nancy because of her rivalry with skater Tonya Harding. Reporters were everywhere, trying to interview Nancy. But I was concentrating on my long program, which I would skate in only two days.

At practice the next afternoon, the top six ladies returning in the final competition were on the ice. I still don't know how it happened, but suddenly I collided with Tanja Szewczenko of Germany. Her skate blade dug deep into my lower leg.

I couldn't believe my eyes as the judges posted my scores for the Olympic short program! My two coaches, Valentine Nicolaj (left) and Galina Zmievskaya (right), were thrilled.

The pain was instant. Never before had I felt anything like it. Blood streamed from the deep gash as I hobbled off the ice. A German doctor gave me three stitches in my leg. He said I also had a slipped disk in my back. He told me I probably wouldn't be able to skate.

I was stunned. Was it over? I wondered. Was my Olympic dream destroyed?

I went in search of Galina. "I want to skate," I told her. "I *must* skate!"

"We will go to practice tomorrow morning," Galina said. "But if there is pain, we will not compete."

The next morning I was afraid to tell Galina how badly my back hurt. I didn't want her to see me cry again. Galina seemed so strong. I wanted to be more like her. But the pain was so great that I broke down in tears. Galina told me to leave the practice session. I refused.

"I don't want you to try to prove how brave you are and then be crippled for the rest of your life," she told me. "You are young. You will skate in the next Olympic Games."

My heart was breaking as I unlaced my skates. Then I spotted Galina standing with the president of the Ukrainian Federation. And I saw the most incredible thing. Galina was *crying*!

I walked over to her, and she tried to hide her tears.

"Galina," I said. "Don't cry. I *can* skate. You will see. I will try my best." Galina hugged me and we left the rink.

At lunch I ate four plates of food! I never eat so much, but that day I didn't care. Galina ate nothing. She was too nervous. During lunch we decided that at the competition I would go out for the warm-up. If I felt okay, I would skate. If I was not okay, I would not skate.

When we returned to the rink, the German doctor gave me two Olympic-approved shots for my pain. I thanked him.

"Don't thank me," the doctor said. "After the competition, you will show me your gold medal."

"Oh, no!" I cried. "I just want to skate. There's no way I can win a medal now." I really didn't believe I had a chance.

The shots made me feel queasy, but my stomach settled down a bit as I circled the ice during the warm-up.

"Are we going to skate?" Galina asked as I stepped off the ice.

"Yes," I answered. "I will not quit now!"

Nancy Kerrigan skated right before me, but I didn't see her program. I was still in the dressing room, pulling on my new pink skating dress. The loud cheers at the end of her program told me she had skated well.

The day before my Olympic long program, another skater and I collided. My leg and back were badly injured. Galina and I thought my Olympic dream was destroyed!

Then it was my turn. The loudspeaker crackled:
On the ice, representing Ukraine...Oksana Baiul!

I had never been so nervous in all my life. Would I be able to land any jumps? Would I be able to skate at *all*?

Galina placed her hand on my shoulder. "Remember, Oksana. Your mama is always with you."

Galina's words made me feel strong again. I skated onto the ice, ready to begin.

I struck my opening pose and lowered my head. I saw nothing but the ice. Only the ice. I told myself, "I can skate well. I *must* skate well."

The familiar medley of Broadway show tunes began. I don't remember anything about the beginning of my routine until my opening jump — a triple Lutz. I landed it perfectly!

The crowd cheered for me, and I realized then that it didn't matter if I *did* fall. The fans just wanted to see me skate. I played to the crowd, and I loved every minute of it.

But as I began my fifth jump, I knew I could not finish the three rotations of the difficult triple toe loop. I had to make it a double toe loop instead. I was near the end of my program now, and there wasn't much time left for me to skate. Nancy Kerrigan's marks had been high — very high.

How much do I want to win? I asked myself. I quickly made a decision. I changed my program and attempted another triple toe loop. This time I landed it!

RIGHT: The cheering crowd raised my spirits as I leaped into a flying spin in my 1994 Olympic long program.

The crowd cheered again. I decided to give everything I had. Instead of finishing with a spin, I added another double jump combination. As I raised my arms in my final pose, emotion swept over me. I started crying from happiness.

I did it! I thought. I actually forgot the pain, and I skated my best.

I stepped off the ice and fell into Galina's arms. "Your mama helped you from up above," she whispered to me.

Galina and I hurried into the kiss and cry with Valentine. Anxiously we awaited my scores. I held my breath. The competition was so close — the closest ever. But five of the nine judges placed me a fraction of a point above Nancy.

"Oksana, you won!" Galina and Valentine cried. "You won the gold medal!"

For a moment, I was stunned. Then I started crying all over again. It was the happiest day of my life. I had dreamed of winning the Olympic gold for so long, but when it actually happened, it was more wonderful than I could ever have imagined.

The Ukrainian national anthem was played for the first time ever at the awards ceremony. I was so proud to have won for my country.

I was sixteen years old, and my dream had come true!

I touched the gold medal and closed my eyes. "This is for you, Mama."

"I did it, Galina! I won the gold medal!"

RIGHT: *Standing on the Olympic podium with silver medalist Nancy Kerrigan (left) and bronze medalist Chen Lu (right).*

My life has changed a lot since the 1994 Olympic Games. The New England town of Simsbury, Connecticut, offered to build a training facility for Viktor and me — the International Skating Center of Connecticut. There would be two rinks and a ballet and weight room. Viktor and I jumped at the chance to train there.

I moved to Simsbury with Galina, her husband, and Galya. Viktor and his wife, Nina, joined us, as did Viktor's brother Vladimir. Olympic pairs gold medalists Ekaterina Gordeeva and Sergei Grinkov also moved to Simsbury. That was before Sergei's tragic death. I will never forget the day Ekaterina called me with the horrifying news that Sergei had died of a heart attack.

I love the rolling green countryside of Connecticut. It reminds me of Ukraine.

He was only twenty-eight years old! Sergei was one of my closest and dearest friends. I will always miss him.

But I am grateful for my many other close friends in America — and, of course, for Slavik. I still talk to him on the phone every week.

I live next door to Galina, who is like a second mother to me. My condo is filled with hundreds of stuffed animals. Most of them were given to me by fans. My dog, a big white-and-brown cocker spaniel named Rudik, lives with me. He understands both Russian and English!

I skate as a professional now, and I skate from my heart. I perform many different programs to many different types of music. What I love best is to skate an entire performance as one character, and to bring my love of ballet to the ice.

Galina and I always try to choose music that tells a story. The Arabian program I performed during the 1995–1996 season was Galina's idea. When I first saw the sketch of my costume, I cried, "Oh, no! I could *never* wear that!"

Galina shook her head. "You are not a little girl anymore, Oksana," she said. "It is time to grow up. It is time to try something new."

Getting ready for an ice show is always exciting—and a little scary. But once I'm on the ice, there's nothing I love more than performing for a crowd.

Galina was right. Soon the program felt perfect for me!

I do not know what other new things the future holds. But I do know that my life will always include skating. I am at peace when I am on the ice. I skate for myself, for Galina, for my fans — and always, for Mama. Years from now, if people still talk about Oksana Baiul, I hope they will remember me as just a normal girl who loved to skate to *Swan Lake*.